Planting a Rainbow

Written and illustrated by
Lois Ehlert

Harcourt Brace & Company
SAN DIEGO   NEW YORK   LONDON

DEDICATED TO SHIRLEY AND DICK

Library of Congress Cataloging-in-Publication Data
Ehlert, Lois. Planting a rainbow.
"Voyager Books."
Summary: A mother and child plant a rainbow of
flowers in the family garden.
ISBN 0-15-262609-3
ISBN 0-15-262610-7 pb
ISBN 0-15-262611-5 oversize pb
[1. Gardening—Fiction.   2. Flowers—Fiction.
3. Mother and child—Fiction.]   I. Title
PZ7.E3225P1   1988   [E]—dc19   87-8528

Printed and bound by Tien Wah Press, Singapore

M L

Printed in Singapore

Every year Mom and I plant a rainbow.

In the fall we buy some bulbs

orange
tiger lily
bulb

TIGER LILY

red
tulip
bulb

TULIP

orange
tulip
bulb

TULIP

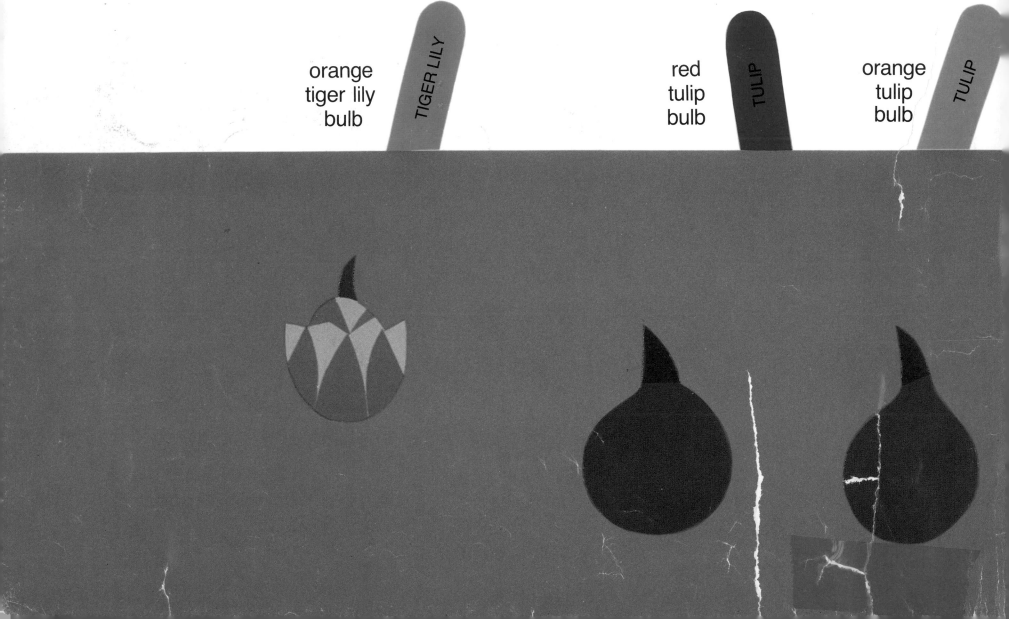

and plant them in the ground.

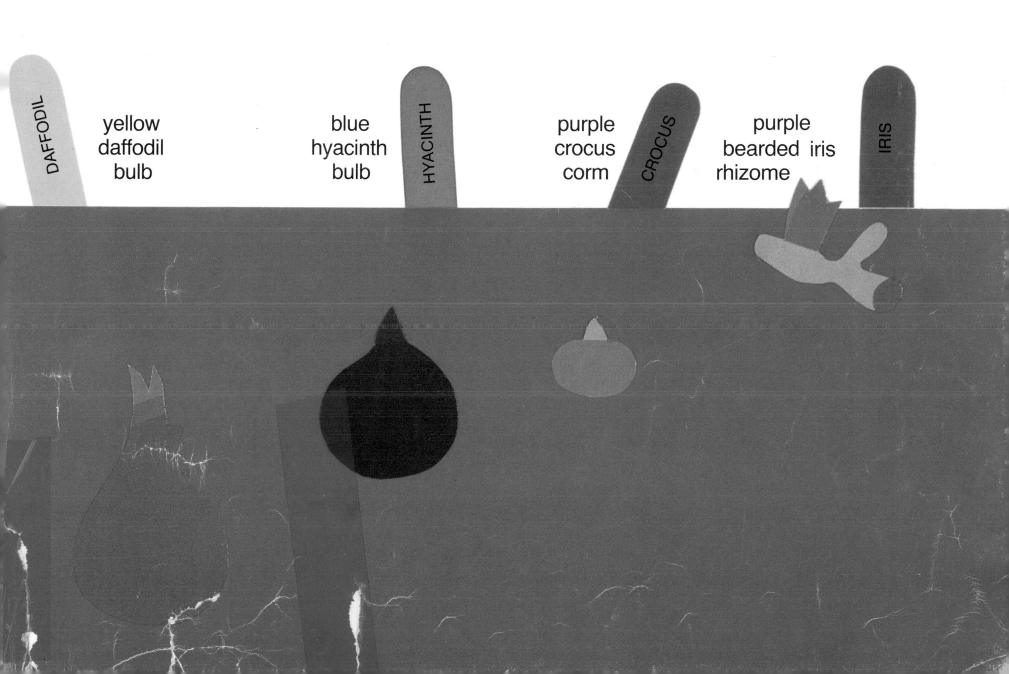

DAFFODIL

yellow
daffodil
bulb

blue
hyacinth
bulb

HYACINTH

purple
crocus
corm

CROCUS

purple
bearded iris
rhizome

IRIS

We order seeds from catalogs and

Phlox

Morning Glory

Zinnia

wait all winter long

Aster

Cornflower

Marigold

Daisy

for spring to warm the soil
and sprout the bulbs.

TULIP

TULIP

DAFFODIL

HYACINTH

CROCUS

Then it's time to go to the garden center to select some seedlings.

We sow the seeds and set out the

TIGER LILY

DAISY

PHLOX

ASTER

CARNATION

ROSE

VIOLET

DELPHINIUM

plants in soil,

MARIGOLD

ZINNIA

MORNING GLORY

CORNFLOWER

IRIS

PANSY

POPPY

FERN

and watch the

ROSE

VIOLET

TIGER LILY

DAISY

CARNATION

PHLOX

ASTER

DELPHINIUM

rainbow grow,

MARIGOLD

ZINNIA

MORNING GLORY

CORNFLOWER

IRIS

PANSY

POPPY

FERN

and grow,

and grow.

carnations

tulips

We have some red flowers

rose

zinnia

and
orange
flowers,

tulip

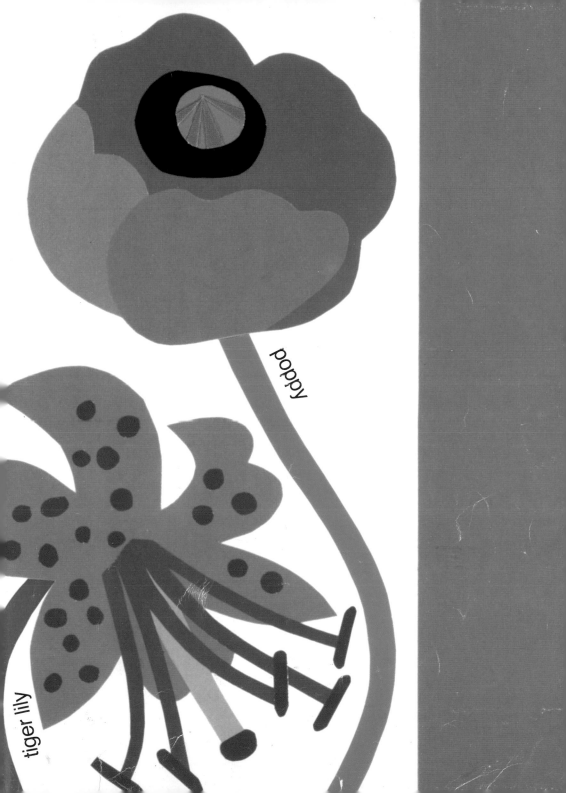

poppy

tiger lily

and some yellow blooms.

daisy

marigold

daffodils

We grow something green

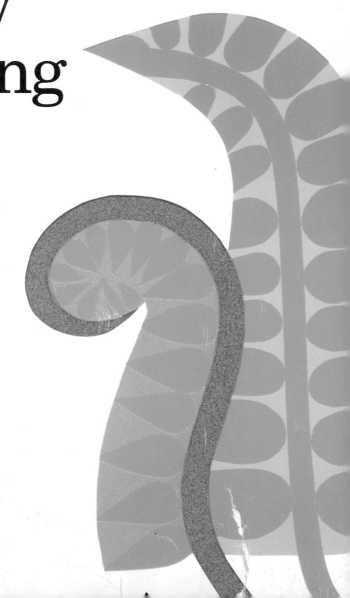

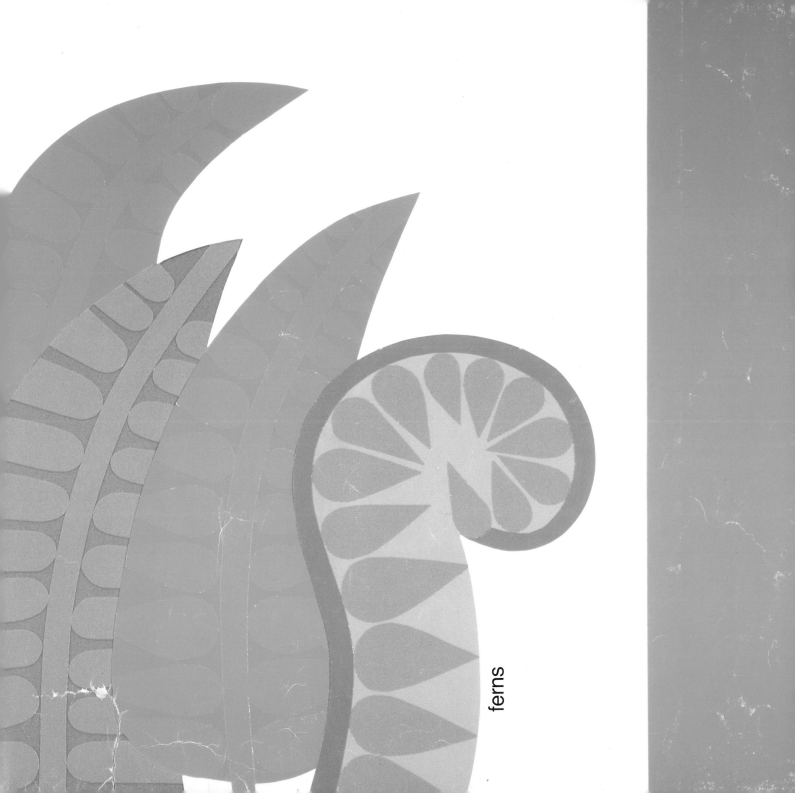

ferns

and
some blue
flowers,

morning
glories

hyacinth

cornflowers

and some
purple
flowers,
too.

crocus

phlox

delphini

iris

violets

asters

pansy

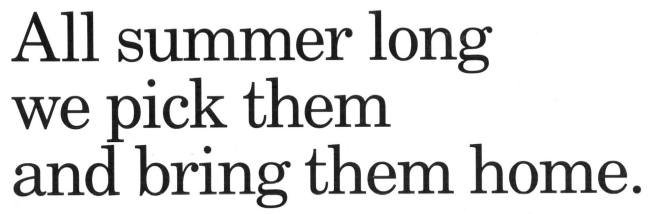

All summer long
we pick them
and bring them home.

And when summer is over, we know we can grow our rainbow again next year.